C:\>010101000111001001111001001000000010011000110111101101111011010110110100101101111001100111001000000010000010110100001100101011000010110010 0BEGINTRANSMISSION...

Try Looking Ahead

Rosarium Publishing
P.O. Box 544
Greenbelt, MD 20768-0544

ISBN: 978-0-9903191-5-3
LCCN: 2014955258

Cover Art: Del Harris
Cover Design: Jason Rodriguez
Interior Art: Stacey Robinson

Try Looking Ahead

Written by Jason Rodriguez
Illustrations by Stacey Robinson
Cover by Dell Harris
Edited by R.S.

This book is dedicated to you.

```
C:\> Rem fontinst.bat
C:\> copy Garamond.ttf %systemroot%\fonts
C:\> regedit /s font.reg
```

Try Looking Ahead

Introductions

In 2036, I was sitting in my bombed-out basement, reading *David Copperfield* through broken glasses. This was after the second Water War, and as far as I knew I was the last person left on earth. If I wasn't, I didn't care enough to find a companion.

I was wrong about that last person left on earth thing.

One day a man entered my bunker, and I instinctively held my hands up to show him that I had enough blood on them already. He held up his and showed me that he didn't have a drop.

He asked me where we were and I told him the *Twilight Zone* and he laughed. I told him it was an old TV show from the sixties. I told him that the show was all about people who found themselves in unexplainable situations. He said he knew the show and that wasn't why he was laughing. He asked what I've dreamt about lately, and I said, "Not this."

He asked me if people still hate each other in this time, and I said, "What people?"

He asked me if I'd like a chance to change the world, and I jokingly said, "Who wouldn't?"

But this man didn't joke.

"What would you do?" he asked me.

I told him where I thought we went wrong. How too many decisions were put into the hands of people who never had to dream. Who always had everything handed to them. Who didn't know anything but the greatest conveniences.

"So how would you change that?" he asked me.

I told him I'd speak to the people who had nothing but dreams and the occasional words on a page to inspire new dreams.

The man smiled and nodded his head and now here I am.

This book was written in the future but constructed in the present. I wrote it for you, in the *Twilight Zone*.

The Boy Who Could See Through Mountains

When Indalecio looked off into the horizon, all he saw was sky and ground, despite the fact that his village is surrounded by mountains. It didn't matter if he turned left or right or looks behind him or didn't turn in any direction at all. Indalecio could only see a straight line that was very far away. On top of that line was the sky; the bottom of that line was the ground. Indalecio never, ever saw a mountain.

His father would point east and say that their friends lived over in that direction. "Two days' walk," he'd say. "Along the river and into the valley." He would point south and say that their vile and evil enemies lived in that direction. "It would be a quick walk to their village if it weren't for the mountain," he'd say.

Indalecio would ask, "Are you afraid? Living so close to our vile and evil enemies?"

"No. There is a mountain between us," Indalecio's father would respond, matter-of-factly. For Indalecio's father, a mountain was a mountain. A mountain was tall and thick and made of rocks. There was really no other way to explain it. Indalecio's father never had to say, "*Look, over there. Do you see that giant rock coming out of the ground? That's a mountain.*" A mountain was one of those things you knew about from a very young age. You may not have remembered the exact moment when you learned what a mountain was, but it was probably the first time you'd ever seen one. Indalecio, however, didn't know what a mountain was because he'd never seen one. He just saw a line off in the distance. On top of that line was the sky. Below that line was the ground.

One day Indalecio was sitting at his kitchen table, eating a plate of eels, when a stray cat pounced on his plate and stole his last bite. Indalecio chased the cat south of the village, through fields of flowers and hopped over rocks and tree roots. The cat continued to run, the baby eel hanging from his mouth and flapping against his face. Indalecio bent over and picked up a rock and threw it at the cat. The rock flew over the cat's head but hit the sky with a *thunk* and rolled back to Indalecio's feet. The cat ran off with the eel, but Indaliecio was more concerned with what made the rock stop in mid-air.

Indalecio picked up another rock and threw it. *Thunk!* It hit the sky and rolled back to him again.

Indalecio walked towards the spot where the sky was hard and stopped when his face smashed against a rock he could not see. He used one hand to cover his bloody nose and the other hand to touch the sky. "This must be the mountain my father told me about," Indalecio said to himself. He couldn't see the mountain, of course, because Indalecio could never see mountains. All he saw was a line in the distance, with the sky on top and the ground below. And a village. Indalecio also saw a village beyond the hard sky. "These must be my vile and evil enemies," Indalecio said.

Indalecio visited the mountain every day. He watched his vile and evil enemies on the other side and waited for them to do vile and evil things. He watched them eat foods that he'd never eaten before and dance in ways that he'd never danced before and wear clothes that weren't like any of the clothes he'd ever worn before. He watched the children play games that weren't like his games. At first the games were terrifying, but after a while they started to look like fun. The food started to look enticing and the dances started to look beautiful and the clothes started to look comfortable. The more Indalecio watched his vile and evil enemies, the more he started to think that they weren't that vile and they certainly didn't seem evil. They seemed perfectly happy on their side of the mountain, just like his people seemed perfectly happy on his side of the mountain.

One day Indalecio asked his father if he ever visited the other side of the mountain. "No," his father replied, "Why would I go there? Our vile and evil enemies live there."

"Have you met any of our vile and evil enemies?" Indalecio asked.

"No," his father replied. "My father warned me about them."

Indelecio asked if his grandfather ever met any of their vile and evil enemies, but Indalecio's father didn't respond. He just ate his dinner, as if no question was ever asked.

Indalecio spent every day in front of that mountain, watching the people on the other side. He wanted to visit the other side of the mountain and try and get to know these people who were supposedly his vile and evil enemies, but he couldn't walk through mountains.

Indalecio would run his hand across the hard sky. He'd push as hard he could, but the mountain wouldn't budge. Since Indalecio couldn't see the mountain, he couldn't comprehend how big it was. How immovable it seemed. No one had ever tried to move a mountain before, the task simply looked impossible. But, to Indalecio, the mountain was nothing but hard sky.

"Maybe one day I can move this mountain," he said to himself.

Reggie & Becky

When Becky was younger, she would play fetch until her body got so hot from all the exertion that she would sometimes pass out. Dogs don't sweat, so if they play too hard their bodies just shut down. And Becky didn't know when to stop—she'd see the ball leave Reggie's hand and take off after it, practically falling over herself as she came upon the ball, legs moving full speed and mouth wide open. And she'd get too hot, and sometimes she'd pass out. But most of the time she'd make it to the ball and pick it up and bring it back to Reggie without passing out. Other times she'd bring it over to a sunny patch of grass and kick it around like a soccer ball. With each round of fetch, she'd start panting louder. Eventually, Reggie would have to stop throwing the ball and show Becky that he was hiding it, otherwise she'd obsess and bark and scratch at Reggie's leg until he threw it again.

That was when she was younger, although it was not fair to say that Becky was ever younger. Reggie's parents adopted Becky when she was eight years old. Becky spent most of her earlier years in the backyard of some owners who would never throw the ball for her.

"She has a lot of catching up to do," Reggie's mom would say, "so make sure you throw that ball for her as much as she can take it."

Reggie would throw the ball for her every day. After school, after Saturday morning cartoons, after Thanksgiving dinner and Christmas morning. In the rain and in the snow and in the extreme heat he'd throw that ball and Becky would chase it down and bring it back.

As the years passed, Becky slowed down. Her legs grew shakier and shakier. Her heart didn't work as well. She'd start coughing after only a few throws.

"She's not the same anymore, mom," Reggie would say, "I want my old Becky back."

"Nothing ever stays the same," Reggie's mom would reply. "This is Old Becky. She'd different than Young Becky."

Old Becky wanted to lie on the couch and watch TV and eat treats. She wanted to snuggle up next to Reggie and have her belly rubbed and be told that she was a good girl. Reggie would do all of this, but he'd also pick up her ball and throw it and watch as Becky's head would turn, excited for a minute, but then she'd lay her head back on a blanket and close her eyes and sleep.

Becky's veterinarian said that she couldn't play fetch any-more because her throat was shrinking. The shrinking throat made it harder to get air and she would cough. The coughing would cause all of these things to happen, but, eventually, her body would turn off and she'd pass out. The veterinarian said there was really nothing they could do about it. Reggie, on the other hand, knew the perfect solution.

He built her a robotic throat, as any kid Reggie's age would do. This throat acted just like any other throat—it swallowed food and took in air and let out air and sometimes let out food, too, if the food wasn't good. It was a bit heavier than Becky's normal throat, being made of metal and all, but Reg-gie thought that was a fair trade-off if it meant she could still play fetch.

Reggie decided to try out his new-and-improved Becky. He threw the ball and Becky took off after it, a little slower than normal, however, because her throat was a little heavier than normal. But she brought the ball back and he threw it again and again and again and she would go and go and go and never cough because her throat was no longer shrinking.

Until one day, when she just watched the ball leave Reggie's hand and, instead of going after it, jumped up, wanting to snuggle.

Reggie and his mom took Becky to the veterinarian again, and this time he said she had a bad heart. He said she was getting old and her heart was getting weaker and it wasn't able to supply Becky with the energy she needed to chase her ball. He said that there was nothing that could be done about this. Reggie, once again, knew the perfect solution.

Reggie built Becky a robotic heart. He found the schematics on BuildARobotHeartForYourDog.com. It was pretty simple, actually. This heart acted just like a normal heart, pumping blood filled with oxygen to the body and taking in blood that was recently filled with new oxygen from the lungs. It was a bit heavier than Becky's normal heart, being made of metal and all, but being a bit heavier seemed like a fair trade-off if it meant being able to play fetch with Becky again.

Reggie was a bit more skeptical this time—he never built a heart before, after all—but he decided to give it a shot, anyway. When he first threw the ball, he was so nervous that Becky's robot heart would fail that he had to close his eyes. But Becky took off after it, quite a bit slower than normal, however, because her heart and her throat were quite a bit heavier than normal. But she would go and go and go and never cough because her throat was no longer shrinking and never got tired because her heart was stronger.

Until, one day, when she chased after the ball and fell. She got up, her legs shaking, and slowly walked over to Reggie and stared up at him, signaling that she just wanted to snuggle.

Reggie didn't want to snuggle, however. He wanted his old Becky back. So he once again took Becky to the veterinarian, and this time the veterinarian said that her legs were getting weak. That the metal throat and the metal heart were putting too much weight on her knees and that her old legs couldn't take the pressure anymore. The veterinarian said that there was nothing they could do about this. Reggie, obviously, knew the perfect solution.

Reggie built Becky robotic legs. The legs could run faster than Becky's old legs and jump higher than her old legs. And when Reggie threw the ball, Becky just watched it leave his hand, walked up to him, and snuggled on his lap.

"Get the ball, Becky!" Reggie shouted, but Becky just looked up at him and waited for Reggie to pet her. "Go get the ball! I'll pet you later!"

Becky never moved.

"Mom," Reggie cried, "Becky doesn't want to get the ball. I don't know what to do!"

"Reggie," his mom replied, "Becky just wants to be an old dog, and she wants to spend her old years with someone who'll pet her."

Reggie knew what he had to do. He took out the robot throat and the robot heart and the robot legs and replaced them with her shrunken throat and bad heart and shaky legs. And he laid down with her all day, petting her belly and telling her she was a good girl.

The next morning, Becky woke Reggie up by licking his face. She seemed different. She seemed younger. "Let's snuggle, girl," Reggie said. But Becky refused. She nudged a ball toward his hand and ran toward the door. Reggie reluctantly followed.

"I can't throw this ball, Becky," he said, "Your throat is too small and your heart is no good and your legs are shaky!"

Becky simply responded by jumping up Reggie's leg, motioning toward the ball in his hand.

"OK," Reggie said, and he gave the ball a little toss. Becky ran after it, picked it up, and brought it back with the speed of a puppy. So Reggie threw it again, this time a little farther, and Becky ran after it, picked it up, and brought it back to Reggie.

He threw it across the yard and Becky brought it back. He threw it down the block and Becky brought it back. He threw it into the park a couple of blocks away and Becky brought it back.

"OK, girl," he said, "This is what you want, so here it comes." Reggie threw the ball as hard as he possibly could. He threw it toward the sunset and never saw it come down.

Becky ran after it, tongue wagging the whole way.

Detective Know-it-All
and the
Glittered-Up Glue Stick

Sally takes a seat at my lunch table. Her long blonde hair's pulled into pigtails that whip this-way and that-way as she scans the cafeteria, making sure no one sees her sitting across from me. She opens her milk and pretends to take a sip, trying to cover up the fact that she's talking to me but garbling up her words in the process. She smells like hamster food. She must be on King Philip duty this week. These secretive cases always give me nerves. I open up my own milk and take a long, hard swig. "Put the milk down," I tell her. "All it's good for is a tummy ache, anyways."

Sally shoots me a dirty look and puts her milk back down on her lunch tray. "I have a problem, and I heard you're the guy who can solve it."

Sally's never said a word to me before this moment, if you don't count the moment before this moment when she tried to talk to me with milk in her mouth. It's the way things go around here—I'm just a fly on a wall until there's a problem that needs to be solved. Then I become a fly on the wall that also solves problems. "I can solve problems, yeah. But I ain't cheap. My fee's two candy bars a day, plus expenses. I prefer Snickers, but as long as it's a full-sized I won't go crying home to my mom. You may have pulled in a great deal of Halloween-sized candy bars last month. You can keep 'em to yourself. People call 'em fun-sized; I call 'em a bad racket. And there's gotta be some chocolate in them, you hear? And nothing too tacky, either. They get stuck between my teeth, and the dentist has been riding me the past couple of visits about flossing."

"That's fine," Sally says a little too quickly. I ask myself why and realize she has a stash of full-sized candy bars in her kitchen pantry. I need to get better at thinking these things through first. I could have easily pushed for four candy bars a day.

She starts to tell me about her problem that needs fixing, but, before she even opens her mouth, I already know that she thinks someone's been taking down her class president posters and replacing them with posters that say things like "Sally Smells" and "Sally Stinks." Kids in the third grade ain't got that great of an imagination, I guess. They understand that things sound better when you use alliteration, that is to say things sound super when someone says sentences by starting words with similar sounds such as "smells" and "stinks" side-by-side with "Sally." So they get poetry points, but they keep using words that refer to Sally's supposed body odor. Lacks imagination and also seems false. As mentioned, Sally smells like King Philip, the class hamster, which means she smells like cedar chips. I like the smell of cedar chips. Who doesn't?

I also know that no one's actually stealing her posters. It's Ricky Ricks (yes, that's his real name), the class bully who's actually making the "Sally Stinks" posters and pasting them over Sally's posters so that he doesn't get caught with a stack of stolen campaign posters in his locker. No evidence, no paper trail—pretty smart for a guy like Ricky Ricks. Not smart enough to outsmart me, however, because there actually is evidence of the crime. The glue stick he's using, which is in his backpack, is covered in glitter—the same glitter Sally uses on her posters.

Now, I know what you're asking. Why does Sally use so much glitter on her posters? No one knows, honestly, but some folks in the school classify her excessive glitter usage as a menace to the grounds. Glitter everywhere. All over the students, the teachers, the desks, the lunchroom. In fact, my vegetable lasagna from yesterday was actually a vegetable and glitter lasagna. I'd call it a glittable lasagna, but I hope to never have to refer to a vegetable lasagna covered in glitter again, as it tastes terrible. Why give it a name, then?

Now, let's back up. I know what you're really asking. You're asking how it is that I know about Ricky Ricks and the poster and the precise location of the incriminating evidence. Well, that's a good question, too. You see, I know everything. I'm a Know-It-All. A real Know-It-All. As in, ask me a question, and I instantly know the answer. And not just stuff in history books. I know what you had for breakfast this morning, what you dreamt about last night (even if you forgot), and what you do after you pick your nose. Don't do that again, kid. That's gross.

I've been like this since I was a baby. I couldn't talk yet, but my mom would say stuff like "Who's the cutest baby?" and a name would pop into my head. Not my name, some kid named Jacob Jackson. He lives in Texas, apparently. He didn't age well. When I ask myself, "Who's the cutest third grader?" his name doesn't even pop up. It's some girl named Michelle from Creston, Iowa. I ask who's the cutest third grader named Jacob, and it's not even him. It's some kid in Israel.

The point of all this is, I know everything. I *literally* know everything. Including the whereabouts of the allegedly stinky Sally's posters and the glittered-up glue stick. And I'm going to officially solve this case...in two days. I need to collect my fee, after all, and two days is four candy bars. Could have been eight candy bars if I asked myself, "Does Sally have a stash of candy bars at her house?" But I didn't, and now I only get four candy bars. But four candy bars is better than no candy bars. There's no use in being a detective if you do the work for free.

"Sally, I don't want you worrying about this. Detective

Know-It-All always gets his man," I tell the nervous Sally. Yeah, I call myself Detective Know-It-All. Who wouldn't in my situation?

Sally seems satisfied with my declaration so I get on the case. And by "getting on the case," I mean I sneak into the back stairwell and read some comic books instead of going to gym. Reading comic books is hard, by the way, when you know everything. You can't think things like, "How's Spider-Man going to get out of this one?" because the second you ask that question you know the answer. "Oh, OK," you say to yourself. "He pulls a lever in Doc Ock's lab that turns on the interdimensional transporter, and Doc Ock gets zapped into the Negative Zone." Once you know how a comic book ends, it's hard to keep on reading it.

Being a Know-It-All isn't as great as you'd think it is. But you learn how to deal with it.

I actually get to the end of one comic book, which is an accomplishment as far as I'm concerned, and I decide to show my face a little bit, make it seem like I'm doing my job. I sneak back into the gym just as a game of dodge ball is coming to an end. I hate dodge ball. You don't have to be a Know-It-All to know how a game of dodge ball turns out. It'll always end with a bloody nose.

I make my way over to Ricky Ricks and ask him if he knows anything about Sally's posters. He gets real angry and threatens to punch me in the nose. I know he won't do it because I know everything, but his response is enough to give me probable cause. I'll grab the glue stick and expose him tomorrow.

After school Sally comes up to me and asks me if I'm making any progress on the case. I tell her I got some suspects and remind her to bring me the candy bars tomorrow. I start to walk away but Sally starts crying and it's hard to walk away from someone when they're crying. I ask her what's wrong, and she responds, "Do you think I smell?"

How do you answer something like that? Fact of the matter is we all smell. Seriously. Some people have a smell on them that no one really notices and some people have a smell on them that other people find offensive but we all smell. When I ask myself, "Does Sally smell?" the answer is, "Yes." But I can't just tell her that.

"I don't think you smell at all, Sally," I say, and I give her a little punch on the shoulder to let her know I'm not lying.

"So why would someone say I smell?" she asks me, and here comes the answer. Ricky Ricks wanted to run for class president but his father wouldn't let him. His father thinks running for class president is something that the Ricks don't do. His father, it seems, was a bit of a bully himself. He doesn't think his son has to beg for friends. "*Ricks don't beg,*" his father says. "*People who beg for friends are weak.*" So Ricky does the only thing his father ever taught him to do—he punishes the people he sees as weak.

All of a sudden I feel bad for Sally. I feel bad for Ricky, too. I ask myself if there's anything I can do to help both of them out and, of course, I get an answer. I don't like the answer, but it's one of those days when you feel the need to do nice things for people who are hurting, I guess.

"Hey Sally, this whole ordeal got me thinking about what you can do if you become President. Look, you're not the only kid in this school who's getting called 'smelly,' right?

Heck, some people are getting called worse. The other day I was called a "toad." A toad! Ugly and slimy and just…I'm not a fan of toads, Sally. Not a fan at all. So, what I'm thinking is…what if you run for president with a team, you know? Some people who could…let's say make a little trouble for folks who call other folks 'smelly' or 'toad' or anything else like that. Assign someone as detective and someone as…I don't know, like an enforcer? You can't call that person an enforcer because the school'll get angry. But someone who can solve the cases and some, you know, muscle to back that other someone up?"

Sally's face lights up because she feels like she has a platform. A real platform. Not something that everyone runs on like "*No More Meatloaf in the School Cafeteria,*" although, if you were to ask me, I'd say that's also a very important platform. "And you would be my detective?" she asks me.

"Well, I'm the only detective in the school. And I am a Know-It-All," I respond.

"And who'll be your…uh…helper?" she asks.

"I was thinking Ricky Ricks. He seems like he got a good heart under all that, you know, Ricky-ness."

Sally laughs and makes it look like she's thinking it over, but I know that she's already decided on what to do. "I think that's a great idea," Sally replies. "I'm going to try to talk to Ricky. Hopefully he's not too…Ricky."

The next day Sally asks me if I've made any progress on the case. I tell her my leads have all dried up and that this could be the one case Detective Know-It-All doesn't solve. It doesn't give her a lot of confidence in my being her go-to anti-bullying detective, but my record's still good despite this recent supposed failure. She still gives me my candy bars, which I'm thankful for, and tells me Ricky's onboard with the plan. "He actually seemed pretty excited about it," she says.

I already knew that, of course.

As the days go by, Sally notices that her posters are no longer missing (or being covered up, which was the real issue). Her glittered monstrosities once again cover the walls, and her anti-bullying message is really working with the students. She has me and Ricky stand behind her when she gives her speeches. She thinks this'll give her plan a bit more weight. Sally seems to think that having Ricky on the team scared the bully that was taking down her posters. She's certainly half-right. Having Ricky on the team certainly stopped her posters from disappearing, but that's only because Ricky found something else to occupy his time. Something that lets him be Ricky, but be Ricky for good reasons.

Sally won in a landslide, Ricky was really happy with his new position, and I picked up two partners. Which is fine and dandy but now I gotta split my candy bars with Sally and Ricky. I'm not particularly fond of that part.

Rocket Ruiz Builds a Warp Drive

Rachel "Rocket" Ruiz won the soapbox derby four years in a row so she was surprised to learn that she wasn't the favorite in this year's race. She perfected the art of soapbox racer building—her car had hardly any drag, was incredibly light, could handle the toughest turns with ease, and had wheels that could spin for hours with one flick of the wrist. She worked tirelessly on her design, experimenting with different materials and lubricants and frames. She kept getting her time down one second at a time and was never satisfied with her personal bests, which she topped every single time. Every year she left her competition in a haze of dust and pebbles. No one ever even came close to beating her. So when everyone started talking about Philip Jones, the new kid in town, and his state-of-the-art soapbox racer, she wasn't nervous… just *curious*.

So she did her research, as any good soapbox racer would. She asked around school to try and get some information on Philip Jones, who didn't go to her school but instead attended the Christopher Academy of Arts and Sciences, a private school on the outskirts of town. As far as Rocket could tell, Philip Jones was the only kid from the town who went to school there. All the other students came from across the country (and even outside the country) to dress up in fancy clothes and learn from the best teachers in the world (at least, according to their website).

Philip Jones' dad was the owner of Precision Automobiles, a company that made very expensive, high-performance car. Precision Automobiles hired the best engineers in the country, and those engineers built cars that sold for more money than Rocket's house was worth. Very rich people would buy these cars and put them in their very large garages alongside other high-performance cars, very slow, old cars, very luxurious cars with umbrellas that popped out of the door, and very large cars with tires that were taller than anyone in Rocket's class.

Although no one ever saw Philip's soapbox racer in action, the rumor was that it was the fastest soapbox racer ever made. It was designed by the best engineers at Precision Automobiles and made from the best, most expensive materials available in the world. Rumor had it that the soapbox racer was lighter than Rocket's, turned better than Rocket's, and was more aerodynamic than Rocket's, and, as a result, could complete the derby course a full ten seconds faster than Rocket's.

Ten seconds may not seem like a lot, but when you consider how much work Rocket put into her soapbox racer, ten seconds could have been ten years. Rocket didn't know how she could compete with a soapbox racer that must have cost tens of thousands if not hundreds of thousands of dollars to build.

But that didn't stop her from trying.

Rocket went to her favorite spot, Dirty Dan's Junkyard, looking for some materials that she could reconfigure into a better, faster soapbox racer. She pulled some fiberglass off of an old Camaro and reshaped it into the perfect soapbox racer body. Stripped off some parts (like her brakes) to make her racer faster but, admittedly, a lot less safe. She experimented with any greasy substance she could find to reduce the friction in her wheels. She tried a design that would have her lying down on her stomach to reduce drag and, when that wasn't fast enough, covered her body head-to-toe in a scuba suit to reduce the amount of wind resistance.

In the five weeks leading up to the big soapbox derby, Rocket tried at least twenty different designs. She hardly slept and rarely ate, thinking that her sickly frame would reduce the weight in the car even more and help her add eleven seconds to her time so that she could beat the new kid, Philip Jones.

However, the best she was able to achieve was eight seconds off of her time. She was still two seconds short of a tie, three seconds short of a win. Not wanting to give up, she decided to try something completely different. She decided to build a warp drive.

Rocket learned about warp drives from watching *Star Trek*, an old TV show about a bunch of guys traveling around in space. You see, when you travel in space, there's only so far a traditional spaceship can take you. Let's say you want to go to a star that's 1,000 light years away. That means that if you did have a traditional spaceship that could somehow travel at the speed of light (which is the fastest a spaceship could *possibly* travel), it would take 1,000 years to get to that star. You would be very, very old by the time you got there. A warp drive is a type of engine that would shrink the amount of space between you and that star, making the star that's 1,000 light years away only a couple of hundred thousand miles away. And, with a spaceship, you could then get there in a couple of days.

Rocket wondered if she could build a warp drive that would shrink the space between the starting line and the finish line. This way, she could finish the race in a matter of seconds. She started doing some research into warp drives. According to her research, no one has ever built a real, working warp drive. Not only has no one ever built a warp drive, but many physicists thought that a warp drive would be impossible to build. And, unfortunately, the physicists who thought a warp drive would be possible to build seemed to think that it would take an astronomical amount of energy to use. An amount of energy so astronomical that it could only be achieved by using something called "dark matter." And dark matter sounded really, really expensive.

Rocket never liked the word impossible, however, and she came up with a design for a warp drive that would allow her to crush Philip Jones. She was sure of it.

The day of the race came and Rocket already had her newly-designed soapbox racer lined up at the starting position. She was sitting in it, looking determined, when Philip Jones pulled up in his fancy, expensive racer.

"So you must be the great Rocket Ruiz?" Philip said with a smug look on his face. "I see you didn't even decide to race today."

It's understandable why Philip would think that. Rocket's race car was, in fact, nothing but a cardboard box with a hole cut out of the top and her head popping out of the hole. There were no wheels. No steering wheel and no brakes. Just a box with the words "DANGER: KEEP BACK TWENTY FEET" scrawled on the sides.

"Oh, no, I'm here to race. And I'm going to destroy your shiny little racer, too," Rocket said, her eyes fixed on the road ahead, particularly the finish line down the hill.

"Well, you left your racer home, it seems!" Philip said with a laugh.

Rocket never looked up at Philip. She kept her eyes on the road and didn't say a word.

"Seriously, Rocket, you're sitting in a cardboard box," Philip said. He wasn't laughing as hard anymore. He sounded a bit concerned. Rocket didn't respond. "I mean, you do realize that, right? You don't even have wheels!"

Philip looked around at the other racers to see if any of them saw what he was seeing. Rocket didn't know how anyone else reacted because her eyes continued to be fixed on the road ahead.

"Rocket!" Philip shouted. "HELLOOOOO? ROCKET?" Philip's unsteady shouts were once again met with silence. "Fine!" Philip yelled, getting into his racer. "Just sit there! I don't care! I was hoping you'd at least put up a fight, but I guess you know you can't beat my racer."

Rocket kept her eyes straight ahead and out of the side of her mouth, she calmly stated, "I built a warp drive."

"A what?" Philip asked, his voice cracking.

"I built a warp drive. You see, you're right. I can't beat your racer. I don't have the money to build a racer like yours. So I built a warp drive."

"What's a warp drive?" Philip's eyes were not on the road. His eyes were on Rocket's racer. He kept reading the warning sign over and over and over. Keep back twenty feet? Why would he need to keep back twenty feet?

"You should watch *Star Trek*," Rocket replied. "A warp drive is a type of engine that'll bring the finish line to me. You can go as fast as you want, it won't matter. I'll be done in less than a second."

Philip's hands shook as he let go of his steering wheel and

turned his entire body to Rocket. "That's impossible!" he shouted. Rocket had once again gone silent. "You're crazy! You can't make the finish line come to you! That's not possible!"

Mr. Robinson, the race organizer, stepped up to the starting line and readied his pistol. The race was just about to start. Philip sat in his racer, staring at Rocket, waiting for her to say anything. Rocket just stared at the finish line.

"Ready your racers!" Mr. Robinson yelled.

"Rocket! ROCKET! A warp drive is against the rules! You can't use a warp drive! ROCKET!" Philip was screaming at the top of his lungs. Rocket was silent.

"ON YOUR MARK!" Mr. Robinson yelled.

"DAD!" Philip shouted toward the stands. "DAD! DAD! ROCKET BUILT A WARP DRIVE! SHE'S CHEATING!"

"GET SET!" Mr. Robinson yelled.

"STOP THE RACE! STOP THE RACE! ROCKET'S CHEATING! SHE'S USING A WARP DRIVE!" Philip shouted toward Mr. Robinson. Rocket was silent.

Mr. Robinson fired his pistol as Philip continued to yell at anyone who would listen. No one was listening. Rocket flipped the switch, releasing the brakes on her racer. Her racer burst out of the cardboard box and started tearing down the hill, leaving all of the other racers behind in a trail of dust and pebbles.

Rocket was a full ten seconds down the hill by the time

Philip realized what was going on. Ten seconds may not seem like a lot, but when you consider the top speed of Philip's racer compared to Rocket's, ten seconds could have been ten years.

Philip released his brakes and started off down the hill, but he never had a chance. By the time he crossed the finish line, Rocket was already celebrating her victory. Philip complained to his dad. He complained to Mr. Robinson. He complained to the other racers. None of his complaining mattered; as far as everyone was concerned (except for his father, of course, who was embarrassed by the fact that his well-financed racer lost to something that was made of scrap parts), he lost the race fair and square.

"This trick won't work next year, Rocket," Philip said. He looked angry. Real angry. Ugly angry.

"That's fine," Rocket replied, "Now I have a full year to build a real warp drive."

Rocket just needed to figure out how to get her hands on some dark matter...

Checking In

In 2015 I was sitting at the Busy Bee Cafe, watching people sip hot coffee without a single understanding of what comes next. I was watching kids cry for candy bars and cookies, baristas roll their eyes when a customer asked for an extra shot of sugar-free vanilla syrup, and two friends sitting across from each other, faces buried in smartphones.

The man from my future came to visit me at the coffee shop, the same man who visited me in my bombed-out basement in 2036.

"How's the book coming?" he asked me.

I handed him my first few stories. He thumbed through them without a word.

Meanwhile, a man bumped into an old lady on the street, spilling her groceries and never once stopping to apologize or offer to help.

The man from my future put the manuscript down, and said, "Finish it."

I don't know how, I replied.

The man from my future looked around and made no attempt to hide his contempt. "You're in the wrong place," he said.

I looked around, confused—coffee shops were where people went to write, everyone knew that.

"You have to go to where the people are," he told me, before getting up and walking out the coffee shop door.

I followed him outside and followed him down the block and around the corner and down two more blocks and around more corners and down more blocks before we got to where the people were.

I saw kids hitting blue bouncy balls with sticks. Throwing basketballs into milk crates. Scratching hopscotch boards into the hot asphalt.

I saw a kid with a model rocket—the other kids were laughing at him, calling him a nerd, until he launched it into the sky—then everyone wanted him to do it again.

I saw a father coming home from a second job, exhausted, but not too exhausted to hug his daughter and hear all about her day.

I saw a mom helping a kid with his math homework.

I saw a bed that was a pirate ship.

I saw a kid playing baseball with his Muppet dolls.

A kid walking home with the violin he borrowed from school.

I told the man from my future that this place looked like my childhood.

"But what's missing?" he asked me.

I didn't know how to respond.

He sighed as if I still had everything to learn, pointed to my manuscript, and said, "This book is what's missing."

I told him that I didn't have this book as a child, either.

"It was missing then, too," he responded. "That's why you were writing in a coffee shop just now, away from the people."

The Monster Hunter

Timmy woke up in the middle of the night to find another monster in his room. The monster was covered in greasy, green hair. The greasy, green, hairy monster had long claws that scraped the floor. It smelled like dirty laundry. Really dirty laundry—football game followed by playing with a wet dog followed by crawling through a sewer dirty laundry. Timmy screamed so loud that everyone in the neighborhood probably heard him, including the greasy, green, hairy, smelly, long-fingernailed monster. It turned toward Timmy. It smiled at Timmy, and its smile was crooked and its teeth were all mangled and filled with little bits of what must have been pieces of human flesh. The greasy, green, hairy, smelly, long-fingernailed, crooked-toothed monster slowly stepped toward Timmy, undoubtedly looking for one last meal. But Timmy's parents barged into the room before the monster made it to the bed, and the monster quietly ducked back into the closet.

"Did you have another nightmare, buddy?" Timmy's father asked. Timmy tried to say something, but he couldn't even respond. He sobbed and sobbed and sobbed and stared at his closet, terrified. He wanted to warn his parents. He wanted to tell them to run out of the house and never come back. He wanted to tell them that the monsters were getting bigger and braver and coming out more frequently these days. That they were uglier and smelled worse and always seemed to have hands filled with chunks of meat or teeth sticky with blood. But he couldn't say any of this—all he could do was cry.

Timmy's mother shut the closet door and looked disapprovingly at the father. "I told you to make sure his closet is closed before bed," she said. "You know how he gets."

"I must have forgotten," the father replied. "Go back to bed. I want to talk to Timmy."

Timmy's father waited for the mother to leave and then walked toward the closet.

"No!" Timmy yelled, but his father ignored him and opened the closet wide. He peeked his head inside, moved some clothes around, and kicked some toys that were on the floor. He ran his fingers along the door frame, turned the light on and off, and knocked on the wall.

"I think the coast is clear," Timmy's father said. He sat back down on the bed, and whispered, "You know, when I was a kid, I had monsters in my closet, too."

Timmy was shocked to hear his father talking about monsters. Adults never talked about monsters. They always said that monsters didn't exist. "You just had a nightmare," they said. That never made Timmy feel better. It made him feel crazy and alone. Hearing his father talk about monsters made Timmy feel like someone understood him.

"What did you do?" Timmy asked. He stopped crying now. He felt a little bit braver. People always feel braver when someone believes them. He puffed his chest out and rubbed his wet eyes on his pajama sleeve and bit his lower lip, but not in a scared way. He bit his lip in a tough way. Like he was saying, "I'm so tough, I bite my own lip because I can."

"Well…it's an old trick your grandpa taught me. You see, what you gotta do is turn your finger into a gun, like this." Timmy's father stuck his thumb in the air and pointed his index finger toward the closet. "And then you gotta say, 'You're dead, monster!' and fire your gun." Timmy's father dropped his thumb down and lifted his hand back, firing an imaginary bullet toward the closet door.

"That won't work!" Timmy said to his father. Timmy thought his father was just telling him kid stuff. There were real monsters in his closet, and fake guns didn't do anything against real monsters.

"It does work, trust me," Timmy's father replied. Timmy felt like a kid all over again. "Next time a monster comes through your closet you just gotta…" Timmy's father made the finger gun motion one more time before leaving Timmy alone in his dark room. Timmy spent the rest of the night staring at his closet. No more monsters came out that night.

———————

The next night Timmy spent an hour looking at his closet before his eyes started to feel too heavy to keep open. He tried to stay awake, but he couldn't fight it any longer. He fell asleep and dreamt of robots. He woke up in the middle of the night to find another monster in his room. A different monster. This one had teeth so long that they poked out of its mouth and rested on its chin. It had scaly skin like a snake. It grunted as it moved across the room. It had fish lips. Timmy screamed again and woke up the entire neighborhood again. The monster started to move toward Timmy, its fish lips puckered and ready to feast. Timmy pointed his index finger toward the monster, raised his thumb, and screamed, "GET OUT OF MY ROOM!" while lowering his thumb and kicking his hand back just like his father showed him.

To Timmy's surprise, the monster dropped to the floor, rolled around for a couple of seconds, and disappeared.

Timmy stopped screaming and looked at his finger gun. His parents ran into his room and his mother closed the closet door, once again yelling at his father for not shutting it earlier.

But Timmy's father just looked at his son and winked.

Timmy wasn't scared of monsters anymore.

——————————

Over the next several weeks, Timmy shot every monster that came out of his closet. He was amazed at how easy it was. One night he saw a monster with big eyes and red feathers. Timmy raised his finger guns, and said, "You ain't flying this coop, pal." Another night he saw a monster with steel armor and breath that smelled like rotting fish. Timmy raised his finger guns and said, "I can STEEL get you, buddy." Yet another night he saw a small monster, sneaking around on tip toes. It tried to run back to the closet when Timmy woke up, but Timmy raised his finger guns fast and said, "At least it's a short fall to the ground, Tiny Tim."

Timmy managed to shoot every monster that came out of his closet for several weeks straight. And then the monsters stopped coming.

——————————

A month passed without any monsters, and Timmy was free to dream of robots and dinosaurs and cars. He got bored, however. He actually had fun shooting all of the monsters that came out of his closet. Shooting monsters made him feel like a hero. Who knew who those monsters were eating when they were out in the world? Timmy was saving lives, and for all he knew the monsters were now coming out of a different closet somewhere else. So Timmy decided to go into his closet and take care of the monsters where they lived.

That night he snuck out of bed and packed his backpack with some food (gummy worms and granola bars), some drinks (chocolate milk and apple juice), some rope from the basement (people always need rope when they go on journeys), and a flashlight from the kitchen drawer. He went back to his bedroom, opened his closet door, and walked into the Monster Kingdom, which was apparently just behind the plaid shirt that he hates. "Makes sense," Timmy said, "Leave it to a monster to hide behind a plaid shirt."

The Monster Kingdom was dark and damp. No clouds were in the sky. No stars, no moon...nothing—just black, damp sky. There was no wind either, and it smelled like sweat and raw meat. Timmy turned on his flashlight. There were piles of mud scattered across the landscape with holes in them big enough for a very tall man (or an average-sized monster) to walk through. Timmy assumed that these were the monsters' houses and walked toward the first one. His finger guns were ready for action.

The house, however, was empty with the exception of pizza boxes and bits and pieces of leftover food. There were no monsters in there.

Timmy walked toward a second house. His hands were shaking. He thought he might be walking into a trap. "What if they know I'm here?" he wondered. "What if they're going to attack me when I'm not prepared?"

The second house had steak bones and candy boxes but no monsters.

The third house had no monsters either. Neither did the fourth nor the fifth nor the sixth house. Timmy checked twenty-eight houses and found that they were all empty. Just scraps of food and trash thrown about.

But the twenty-ninth house was not empty.

In the twenty-ninth house there was a small monster lying on the floor, sleeping. It had huge hands (especially for a small monster) and horns on its head, and its skin looked slimy. Timmy said, "Wake up, monster!" holding his finger guns toward the beast. The monster woke up and screamed. Its scream probably woke the entire Monster Kingdom. For the first time in his life, Timmy looked into a monster's eyes and saw something he never expected to see. The monster was scared of him.

The monster continued to scream until a bigger monster entered the room. This monster also had huge hands and horns and slimy skin. Timmy turned his finger guns toward this monster, expecting to be attacked. Instead, it ran toward the smaller monster, blocking it from the path of Timmy's finger guns.

The bigger monster's eyes were wide and terrified and wet. It made odd noises that sounded sad and terrible.

Timmy didn't know what to do. He looked at the monsters and he looked at his finger guns and he couldn't bring himself to lower his thumb. Instead, he just ran. He ran out of the house and found hundreds of monsters standing by, looking to see what was going on. When these monsters saw Timmy, they also started to scream. They ran from him so fast that they started falling over each other. Timmy chased after them, not to shoot them with his finger guns (which he put away at this point), but to calm them down. Nothing he did calmed them down, however. He tried to smile. He tried to hold his hands out to show them that he didn't want to hurt them, but this just made them more terrified of him.

Timmy ran after them until something caught his eye. It was a piece of paper attached to the side of one of the mud houses. He couldn't read what it said, but it looked like a wanted poster. The type of poster that you would see in old cowboy movies. There was a drawing of a person on the poster. The person looked mean and vicious. The person looked like he wanted to hurt everyone in the Monster Kingdom and would stop at nothing to make sure that there were no more monsters left.

It was a picture of Timmy.

Timmy looked toward the terrified monsters. Most of them were still running, but a few were watching him from a distance. They looked defeated. They looked tired and hungry. They look scared. Timmy looked back at the poster, looked at his face, and saw how these monsters saw him.

Timmy held his head low, turned to the monsters, and whispered, "Sorry." He took the food out of his backpack—the granola bars and gummy bears and chocolate milk and apple juice—and placed it all on the ground. "I hope you found another way to my world," he said. "If not, you can come through my closet again. I won't hurt you." The remaining monsters looked at Timmy inquisitively. They didn't understand a word he was saying. Timmy went back into his room. He left his closet door open and lay back on his bed. After an hour of tossing and turning, Timmy finally fell asleep.

Timmy dreamt of monsters that night.

He never saw a monster again, however.

The End of Stars

Jessie was lying in the grass, giving names to stars, when the sky first began to fall. There were no clouds in the sky. No canopy of trees. No cliffs nearby with pebbles shook loose by squirrels. No birds flying by or boys off in the distance, throwing acorns at Jessie as they usually did. The piece of sky that fell wasn't a shooting star or a meteor. It wasn't hail or a clump of pollen from a nearby patch of wildflowers. It wasn't spittle from Mr. Maguire, Jessie's English teacher, who shot saliva from his mouth every time he said "this" or "that" or "the other thing" (the last phrase being the culprit behind three bursts of rapid-fire spit). And it certainly wasn't Jessie's imagination. The piece of sky that fell next to her head just as she was naming this one particularly bright star "Geronimi" (a name she decided meant "Little Geronimo" in Italian) was smooth like glass, transparent, and sharp like a razor. It was, without a doubt, a piece of the sky simply because there was nothing else it could have possibly been.

Jessie picked up this smooth, transparent, sharp piece of sky and ran back into her house screaming, "Momma! Momma! The sky is falling!" She ran through her door so hard that the whole house shook. This wasn't to say that Jessie was particularly strong (although she wasn't weak, mind you); but it is to say that her house was made of old wood, and old wood shakes with even the slightest bit of force. This is an important point because there was absolutely no way Jessie's old, wooden house could have withstood a falling sky.

Jessie's mother and father were sitting at the kitchen table, playing a card game that only parents play. It's called cribbage. Do not worry about the rules of cribbage; you will only need to learn them if you ever become a parent. Jessie's parents jumped when the old, wooden house that could never withstand a falling sky shook, and they dropped their cards onto the old, wooden, and, frankly, quite dirty floor.

"Jessie!" her father said. "You can't go around banging doors and walls! It's against the rules!"

Jessie didn't much care about arbitrary rules just then. She ignored her father, and shouted, "Dad! Look! It's part of the sky! It fell while I was naming stars!"

Jessie's father laughed. Jessie's mother pinched her cheek, and said, "You're so imaginative sometimes!" Although Jessie was, indeed, imaginative sometimes (something she was proud of, in fact) she didn't think she was being complimented at this exact moment.

"I'm serious!" Jessie screamed. "There was nothing else around me! I was the only person, place, or thing in between the grass and the stars! I saw it falling down, and it almost hit me! It would have cut me, look at how sharp it is!"

Jessie's parents took the smooth, transparent, and razor sharp piece of sky out her hands and observed it very closely. It was unlike anything they'd ever seen before. It was smooth like a rock on the beach, but it seemed much more fragile than a rock. It was transparent like the water in the well, but it didn't fall apart when you tried to pick it up. It was sharp like the scythe they used to clear the fields but it pricked them when they touched the edges ever-so-lightly and the scythe was never that sharp. It was, without a doubt, a piece of the sky simply because there was nothing else it could have possibly been.

Jessie's parents ran to Mayor Fredrickson's house with the smooth, transparent, sharp piece of sky in their hands while screaming, "The sky is falling! The sky is falling!"

Mayor Fredrickson came to the door in his pajamas. He had chocolate on his thick mustache, much like he always did. Mayor Fredrickson always ate chocolate, even when he was sleeping. "What is the meaning of this racket?" Mayor Fredrickson asked Jessie's parents, who were standing on his porch and breathing heavy, holding the smooth, transparent, and sharp piece of sky in their hands.

"Mayor Fredrickson! Look! It's part of the sky! Jessie saw it fall while she was naming stars!"

Mayor Fredrickson looked annoyed. He looked back into his house as if a piece of chocolate was calling his name, turned back to Jessie's parents, and said, "That's ridiculous! The sky can't fall! It's the sky!"

Whereas that argument made sense to Jessie's parents, they still insisted that Mayor Fredrickson look at the smooth, transparent, sharp piece of sky that Jessie found. Mayor Fredrickson turned the piece of sky over in his hands. It was smooth like a baby's cheek, but it certainly wasn't made of skin. It was transparent like the air, but it didn't move up his nostrils, carrying the smell of melted chocolate. It was sharp like a dagger, but no one would be able to use this as a weapon. It was, without a doubt, a piece of the sky simply because there was nothing else it could have possibly been.

Mayor Fredrickson took the piece of sky into his house and ate one last piece of chocolate because it helped him think. He came back outside, held his chest out, and made a decree. "I have decided that this is definitely the sky," Mayor Fredrickson told Jessie's parents. "I hereby decree that the sky falling down is a terrible situation, one that would crush our village. How to best handle this situation, however, is not something I am equipped to answer. We must take this piece of sky to Mr. Collins. He will know what to do next."

Mr. Collins was the village's science teacher. He knew all about what made fire hot (magic) and what made water wet (sprites) and what made grass green (the sun) and what made trees tall (love) and what made boats float (magic, again) and what made chocolate delicious (something he called "quick spots") and what made "quick spots" quick (magic, of course). Mayor Fredrickson ran to Mr. Collins' house, holding the smooth, transparent, and sharp piece of sky above his head, screaming, "The sky is falling! The sky is falling!"

Mr. Collins was wide awake. He never slept. He invented a drink called Wake-a-Lot that made it so he was never tired. This way, he could carry out his experiments. Today he was trying to discover what made the clouds rain. It was his working theory that the clouds got sad when people told bad jokes. He enlisted the help of Phillipe Papadapacristopa Dudeo the Second, the worst comedian in the village. His real name was Jim. He called himself Phillipe Papadapacritopa Dudeo because he thought it sounded funny. As mentioned, he was the worst comedian in the village.

"BE! QUIET!" Mr. Collins yelled at Mayor Fredrickson, "WE'RE CONDUCTING AN EXPERIMENT!" Mayor Fredrickson stopped dead in his tracks, the smooth, transparent, and sharp piece of sky held in his hand. "Please proceed, Mr. Dudeo," Mr. Collins said to the worst comedian in the village.

"Hey, clouds!" Mr. Dudeo yelled to the sky. Mayor Fredrickson noticed there were no clouds in the sky, but he realized that he knew nothing about how science worked. "Why did the chicken cross the road?"

The sky, with its lack of clouds, was silent.

"To get away from the other chickens!"

Mayor Fredrickson didn't get the joke, but he also realized that he knew nothing about comedy, even bad comedy.

The sky was silent, as was Mr. Collins, as was Phillipe Papadapacristopa Dudeo. "Excuse me, Mr. Collins," Mayor Fredrickson began saying before being shushed by Mr. Collins.

"What part of SCIENCE don't you understand, Mr. Mayor?" Mr. Collins said in that way teachers speak when their students are acting up.

"All of it," thought Mayor Fredrickson.

The three men stood outside of Mr. Collins's house, waiting for a cloud (which wasn't in the sky) to open up and start raining after hearing Phillipe Papadapacristopa Dudeo's terrible joke. And they waited. And waited some more. "Tell another one, Mr. Dudeo," Mr. Collins said.

"Mr. Collins, if I could just…"

"SCIENCE!" Mr. Collins shouted, cutting off Mayor Fredrickson once again.

"LOOK!" Phillipe Papadapacristopa Dudeo shouted, pointing up to the sky. A large piece of *something* was falling. It didn't look like rain. Nor did it look like hail or pebbles or pollen or acorns or anything a bird would drop. It hit the ground with a reasonable *thump*. It was smooth, transparent, and razor sharp.

"Mr. Collins! How long have you been out here conducting this experiment?" Mayor Fredrickson asked.

"For about five hours, I'd say. What in the world was that?"

Mayor Fredrickson showed Mr. Collins the piece of smooth, transparent, and razor sharp sky that Jessie found and said, "It's *this*! This is what I came to tell you about, Mr. Collins! The sky *is falling*! It's obvious your experiments are causing it to break apart!"

Mr. Collins started to say that Mayor Fredrickson's conclusions were ridiculous, but just then another chunk of sky fell. And another. And another.

And that's when everyone in the village began to scream, "The sky is falling! The sky is falling!"

A piece of sky fell on Mr. and Mrs. Tucker's barn. It was a large piece, about the size of a cow. "The sky is falling! The sky is falling!" screamed Mr. and Mrs. Tucker.

Another piece of sky fell and destroyed Old Man Deskins' cart. "The sky is falling! The sky is falling!" screamed Old Man Deskin.

A gigantic piece of sky fell in the middle of Flannery's Valley, leaving a giant crater. This caused everyone within earshot to run out of their houses, screaming, "The sky is falling! The sky is falling!"

Everyone was running around and screaming, but no one knew what to do. People were digging holes, climbing trees, and jumping in lakes, but nothing could protect them from the falling sky. One by one the stars went out as pieces of sky plunged to the earth. And one by one the villages began to scream for help, their voices adding to the sound of crashing sky. Pieces of the moon began to crumble to the ground, as well, and the village was becoming darker with each passing moment.

"People!" a voice bellowed through the air, "You *must* follow me!" The voice was coming from Crazy Bill, the eccentric old hermit who lived on the outskirts of town. His clothes were always tattered and his hair was always a mess. Mr. Collins said he was a witch, able of conjuring magic spells in his basement and always experimenting with odd-colored liquids and pieces of metal. He held a device to his mouth that wasn't like anything the villagers have ever seen. It fit in one hand yet made his voice sound like thunder. It was a very commanding voice. The kind of voice you can't ignore.

So the villagers began to follow Crazy Bill as he ran toward the forest, trying to escape the falling sky.

They got to a rocky path that headed up toward Mount Wells, the mountain that everyone knew was impassable because they'd been told it's impassable since birth. No one stopped to complain or question their path, however, as Crazy Bill was the only one telling them what to do. As they ran along the path, which was getting steeper and steeper, some villagers would stop and turn and watch as their houses were destroyed by the falling sky.

Phillipe Papadapacristopa Dudeo was upset because his jokes were apparently so bad that they caused the sky to fall. Mr. Collins felt like a failure because he spent all of his life in the pursuit of science without ever wondering if what he was doing was right. Mayor Fredrickson was mainly worried about all of his chocolate, which would surely be lost to the falling sky. Jessie's mother and father, however, were worried about

Jessie, who was nowhere to be found.

"Crazy Bill! Wait!" Jessie's father shouted. "My daughter! I don't know where my daughter is!"

Crazy Bill frowned, put the thunder voice thing to his mouth, and shouted, "Everyone keep walking up this path. Do not turn back!" He put the thunder voice thing down, and said to Jessie's parents, "That means you, too. I'll get your daughter. I know where she is."

Jessie's parents didn't question Crazy Bill. Instead, they continued to run up the path toward the top of Mount Wells. Crazy Bill went back down the path at a relaxed pace. He saw Jessie down at the start of the path on the outskirts of the forest. She was looking up at the sky, saying goodbye to all of the stars she named. Geronimi just fell to the ground, and for some reason this one made her especially sad.

"You always were a smart one," Crazy Bill said to Jessie. Jessie was crying now. She knew that she would never see the stars again.

"Why isn't the sky falling right here?" she asked.

Crazy Bill put his hand on Jessie's shoulder, sighed, and said, "Because there is no sky here. The sky ended a bit aways from here."

Jessie looked at Crazy Bill. She was confused, obviously, because it's not possible that the sky could end. Of course, she thought this while watching the sky fall on top of her village and realized that everything she always thought she knew about the sky was probably wrong.

"Jessie, I was hoping to teach you all about the sky when you were a bit older. But it seems like I don't have a choice anymore." Crazy Bill didn't sound crazy at all right now. He sounded sad. Maybe even scared, but a different kind of scared compared to the villagers.

"What about the sky?" Jessie asked.

"When I was a little older than you, ten, maybe, this crazy old hermit from the outskirts of town named Steven pulled me out of school and said he's going to be my teacher from now on. He said I was real smart and inquisitive and that I shouldn't be learning about magic and quick spots. He said I should be learning about science. Turns out, some crazy old hermit who lived on the outskirts of town pulled him out of class when he was ten and said the same thing. And some other crazy old hermit pulled that crazy old hermit out of class. This, apparently, has been going on for thousands if not tens of thousands of years. Crazy old hermits pulling kids out of school and teaching them to become crazy old hermits."

Jessie thought she was confused before, but that was only because she didn't understand why the sky would fall. She was very, very confused now.

"I was going to pull you out of school when you were ten, Jessie, in order to teach you about the sky. About where we came from. I was going to turn you into a hermit so that you could one day pull some other ten-year-old out of school."

"I'm sorry, Crazy Bill..."

"Please, call me Bill," Crazy Bill said.

"I'm sorry, Bill, but I have no idea what you're talking

57

about."

Crazy Bill smiled and pushed his shoulders back and looked back up the path. "I believe it's best if I show you, Jessie," he said.

Jessie turned around one last time and saw that most of the sky had fallen. The moon was just a few pieces of light, and the stars were all but gone. "OK," Jessie said, and she turned toward the path with Crazy Bill, her shoulders not as straight as his but her eyes as worried as his seemed to be. "What's up there?" she asked.

"Truth is, Jessie," Crazy Bill said, "I have no idea. I was always told it was too dangerous to go up the mountain until the time was right. Well—it looks like the time is now right."

Jessie and Crazy Bill walked up the dark path in silence. It was a difficult climb that got steeper and steeper. The rocks beneath their feet would slip on occasion, causing one or both of them to fall to their knees. They pushed on, however.

Eventually they got to a place where the land leveled out every 18 inches or so. It was much easier to walk up this part of the path, which felt more like metal than rocks and dirt. "These are called stairs," Crazy Bill said to Jessie. That word meant nothing to her.

They then reached the side of the mountain that was too steep to climb. It was tall and flat and smooth. The villagers were all there, trying to move farther, but they kept bumping into the tall, flat, smooth piece of mountain.

"Just stand back," Crazy Bill responded. "What you're about to see…well…it's only been described to me. You see, a long,

long time ago, humans destroyed the sky. Not the way our village's sky was just destroyed. They did it in a manner much different, but they did it all right. The sky was a combination of wind and rain and fire. People were…well…there were a lot of people back then. A couple of smart folks found a way to live underground. They built our village and our sky. Learned how to plant. Figured we'd need to stay there for many generations so it was best to get into the habit of not telling folks. But, well, here we are."

"Where?"

"About to go outside, the real outside, for the first time in a long, long time."

"What does it look like?"

"Honestly? I have no idea. But you best stand back."

Crazy Bill pushed a rock that was protruding from the tall, flat, smooth piece of mountain. Jessie watched as a crack began to form in the mountain. A completely straight crack that opened wider and got brighter with every passing moment. The light was so bright that it stung her eyes. Jessie never saw anything like it before in her life. "What is that?" she said, burying her eyes into her arm to shield herself from the light.

"It's a star," Crazy Bill said. "The brightest star you've ever seen."

"What's it called?" Jessie asked.

"How about you name it, Jessie? I hear you're good at that."

The Girl Who Could Live In Yesterday

Everett jumped on the table and devoured Macy's birthday cake. "No, Everett!" Macy shouted. But it was too late. Everett gobbled every last bite and ran away with his tail between his legs.

Macy started to cry because she really liked birthday cake. Her mom patted her head, and said, "It'll be OK. I'll make another cake tomorrow."

"Tomorrow isn't good enough!" Macy shouted. "I want birthday cake on my birthday!"

Macy ran into her room, plunged her face into her pillow, and cried. Everett came in to comfort her, but Macy shouted, "Go away, you dumb dog! You ruined my birthday!"

Later that evening, Macy's dad came into her bedroom. He asked Macy if she had seen Everett. Macy responded, "I don't want to see that dumb dog!" Macy's dad looked worried because Everett wasn't in the house. "He might have run away," Macy's dad said. Macy didn't know how to respond, so she simply buried her head back into her pillow.

As Macy lay there crying, she began to ask herself questions. Why did she tell the dog to go away? Why did she call him dumb? Macy's dad saw how upset she was, and said, "I'm sure she didn't go far. Let's go look for her." That sounded like a good idea so she walked around the neighborhood with her dad and mom, calling Everett's name.

"Everett!" she yelled. "Come back! I didn't mean what I said! You're a good dog! You're not dumb! Please come home, Everett! I'm sorry! I'm so sorry! If I could take it back I would! Just please come back!"

They never found Everett.

"Tomorrow we'll make posters," Macy's mom said.

Macy didn't want to make posters. She just wanted Everett back. Before going to bed, she wished that she could live today all over again. If she could live today over again, she'll fix her mistakes. Even if Everett ate her birthday cake, she'd hold him and tell him that it was OK. She'd make it so that he'd never want to run away. She'd make everything right.

When she woke up the next morning, Everett was in bed with her, and her mom was standing over her bed.

"Everett came back!" Macy exclaimed.

Macy's mom just laughed. "Everett never left, silly," she said. "And happy sixth birthday, by the way!"

Macy was confused, because she clearly remembered Everett running away last night. "Maybe I dreamt that," she said. It wouldn't be the first time Macy mistook a dream for something that actually happened.

That night Macy's mom put the birthday cake on the table. Everett lunged for the cake but Macy, prepared for this possibility after last night's dream, held him back. She gave him a treat, and said, "You can't have cake, Everett. Cake isn't good for you anyway!"

Later that evening, Macy's dad came home from walking Everett. "Macy," her dad said. "Don't get upset, but Everett got off of his leash. We have to go and find him."

This whole thing seemed familiar to Macy. Just like in last night's dream, Macy, her mom, and her dad walked all over the neighborhood looking for Everett, and, once again, they couldn't find him. But this felt different than her dream. This time it had nothing to do with what she said. It had nothing to do with Everett eating cake or her calling Everett "dumb." She didn't do anything wrong, unlike in her dream, and yet Everett still ran away. She didn't know why.

When they got back to the house, Macy's mom said, "Tomorrow we'll make posters."

Everything felt too familiar to Macy, and she wondered if she actually did get a chance to do everything over. If her dream wasn't actually a dream but if she actually woke up in yesterday. That seemed like a possibility.

"If I get a chance to try again, I'll walk Everett with dad," Macy said to herself.

The next morning she woke up to find Everett in bed with her and her mom in her room wishing her a happy sixth birthday. Macy didn't even care that it was her birthday for a third time. She hugged Everett, and said, "You won't get away this time!"

Macy spent the day at school thinking about how she wouldn't let Everett eat her birthday cake and how she would walk Everett with her dad that night so he wouldn't escape.

When Macy got home from school, however, her mom told her that Everett ran away. Apparently, Macy left her window open, and Everett must have crawled through it. They walked through the neighborhood again, shouting his name. But deep down, Macy knew that they wouldn't find Everett. But

Macy also knew that she'd have another chance to fix this all tomorrow.

"Tomorrow we'll make posters," Macy's mom said.

Macy knew that they wouldn't make any posters tomorrow.

The next morning Macy woke up with Everett in bed with her and her mom wishing her a happy sixth birthday. "Mom, I don't feel well," Macy said.

Macy stayed home from school. She locked herself in the room with Everett. That night Macy had birthday cake and held Everett back. She went with her dad on Everett's nightly walk. But later that evening, a storm cloud formed over Macy's house. Lightning flashed and scared Everett. He ran out the back door, which was left opened, and across the porch and into the streets.

"Tomorrow, I'll make sure all of the doors are closed," Macy said to herself.

Ten years later, Macy woke up for the three thousandth, six hundredth, and fifty-fifth time. She hugged Everett, and her mom once again wished her a happy sixth birthday, which seemed ridiculous because when Macy looked in the mirror she didn't look like she was six years old. She looked like she was 16, in fact.

Macy stayed home from school and shut her windows and locked her door and tried hard not to make any loud noises that would scare Everett off (like he did the two hundredth and second time she relived yesterday) and made sure Everett didn't sneak out of her room and out of the house when she went to the bathroom (like he did the three-hundredth and sixty-sixth time she relived yesterday) and kept him away from her birthday cake and went on a walk with her dad and locked all the doors in the house and did everything else she possibly could in order to stop Everett from running away for the three thousandth, six hundredth, and fifty-sixth time. But this time her grandmother came by for a surprise visit, and, when the door opened, Everett ran outside again.

"Tomorrow I'll call grandma early so she doesn't have to come by," Macy said to herself.

Thirty years later, Macy woke up for the fourteen thousandth, six hundredth, and thirteenth time. She hugged Everett and her mom once again wished her a happy sixth birthday. Macy definitely did not look like a six-year-old. She was clearly older than her mom at this point.

Macy stayed home from school and barricaded her windows (so Everett couldn't crash through them when the garbage truck backfired like it did the two thousandth, eight hundredth, and eighty-fifth time she relived yesterday) and locked her door and refused to go to the bathroom and took all of her toys off of the shelf (so that they wouldn't fall off and frighten Everett so much that he broke her door down like he did on the three thousandth, two hundredth, and thirty-fifth time she relived yesterday) and refused to eat and kept Everett on a leash and unplugged the television (so the volume wouldn't scare Everett again) and called her grandmother and called her teacher so that she could get the homework she missed before he decided to stop by (giving Everett an opportunity to escape again) and kept Everett away from her birthday cake and asked her mom not to use the garbage disposal (so it wouldn't frighten Everett again) and cleaned up the pizza that someone dropped near the house (so Everett wouldn't break free of his leash trying to eat it again) and carried a rock that she could throw at the squirrel (so Everett wouldn't try to chase it and get off of his leash again) and went on a walk with her dad and locked the doors and did everything else she possibly could in order to stop Everett from running away for the fourteen thousandth, six hundredth, and fourteenth time. But this time the radio said that a tornado was coming and that everyone needed to evacuate their houses. In the confusion, Everett escaped.

It seemed to Macy that maybe the circumstances surrounding Everett escaping were getting more and more ridiculous. At the same time, she knew that she would have another chance to prepare for this possible escape when she woke up once again in yesterday.

"Tomorrow I'll break the radio," Macy said to herself.

Thirty more years later, Macy woke up for the twenty-fifth thousandth, five hundredth, and seventieth time. She hugged Everett with her weak arms, finding it hard to lift them like she used to, and her mom once again wished her a happy sixth birthday. Macy wanted to scream, "Mom, look at me! I'm not six! I'm obviously not six! I'm older than you, mom!" But she knew it wouldn't make a difference. Despite how old she was, she'd been living in yesterday her entire life, and yesterday she was always six. Yesterday, she was always trying to stop Everett from running away despite the fact that Everett had always found a way to run away.

Macy's bones ache, and she now had a hard time keeping Everett in her room. These days, Everett always ran away within hours of waking up. She didn't even try to stop him anymore. She just played with him until he decided to escape. At least tomorrow, which would be yesterday all over again, she would have a chance to play with him again. Even if it was just a little bit.

That night, after twenty-five thousand, five hundred, and seventy-one repeats of yesterday, Macy decided that she was going to make posters the next morning. Whereas it was fun having some time with Everett every morning, yesterday had become too painful to live yet again. For the first time in a long time, Macy didn't ask to do the day over again. She let go of yesterday and fell asleep.

Macy woke up for the twenty-five thousandth, five hundredth, and seventy-second time, and Everett wasn't in bed with her. Her mom didn't wish her a happy sixth birthday. Instead she stayed home from school to make posters. They hung the posters all over the neighborhood, but Macy was so old now that it took all the energy out of her. She went home and took a nap.

Three hours later, Macy felt a wet tongue on her face. She woke up to find Everett standing over her, slobbering on her sheets and nudging her to get out of bed. "Nick from next door found her," Macy's mom said. "I told you she'd be OK."

Macy hugged Everett and cried happy tears. "I'm so happy you're home!" Macy said. "I'm going to spend every day petting you from now on!"

But Everett was a puppy and Macy was old and she just didn't have the energy to play with him anymore.

Anita's Dreams

Anita watched as a T-Rex tried to catch a fast little dinosaur. The fast little dinosaur heard the T-Rex's heavy feet as the T-Rex plodded through the jungle, knocking over trees and scattering every living thing that happened to be near him. His stubby legs couldn't match the speed of the fast little dinosaur, and his tiny arms waved around as if he were trying to catch a cab and was failing miserably. The T-Rex gave up after a minute and roared, frustrated by another lost meal.

The roar was sad because the T-Rex sounded miserable and hungry, but it was also frightening. It startled Anita. She woke up in her bed, sweating and breathing heavily, happy to be home again, but wishing that she could find some way to help the T-Rex. Maybe cook him some pasta with eggplants. Teach him to eat vegetables since vegetables won't run away.

Anita joined her mother for breakfast and told her about her dream. Anita's mother loved to hear about Anita's dreams—they were always filled with interesting little facts and bits of imagination. Anita's dreams were more exciting than her mother's typical day, which was full of worry and work. After hearing about Anita's dream and laughing at the T-Rex, Anita's mother drove Anita to school and then headed to her job at the post office.

Anita didn't have many friends in school. All of the kids talk about music they were hearing on the radio, but the only music Anita had was her mother's old records. No one in school cared about Anita Baker (who Anita was named after) or Sam Cooke. They all liked these singers who'd only been around for a couple of years and most likely wouldn't be around next year. Anita had tried to listen to popular music but never understood why people liked it. It all sounded like a math equation to her, and she hated math.

In one of Anita's dreams, she saw Sam Cooke play at a place called the Copa. She told her mother all about the dream, and her mother told her that the Copa was an old nightclub in New York and that Sam Cooke did play there. Twice, in fact. She said it was a tremendous achievement for an artist like Sam Cooke to play at a place like the Copa, although Anita didn't understand why. Her mother explained that Sam Cooke was a black man and back then black men didn't usually get to play at places like the Copa. Anita said she didn't know any of this, and her mother thought it was all a weird coincidence.

In science class, Anita's teacher continued his lesson on dinosaurs. He made a joke about how the T-Rex was probably a terrible hunter. He was just too big and probably too slow. His short arms made it difficult to grab things. It was likely that he just ate animals that already died, instead of hunting them.

As usual, Anita's dreams seemed very accurate to her. As usual, she mentioned this to no one, as mentioning it made people laugh at her.

Anita always seemed to dream about things that really happened, even if she never knew they happened. Like the time she saw President Lincoln give a speech. She had this dream after her teacher taught them about slavery. Anita thought slavery sounded like a terrible thing, which it was. Anita's mother told her that the world had changed a lot since then, but nothing ever changed all at once. Her mother looked upset, kind of like the T-Rex who couldn't catch the dinosaur no matter how hard he tried. Anita didn't understand what her mother was talking about, but that night she dreamed about President Lincoln. He was talking about ending a war that was being fought to free the slaves, but it didn't sound like he was talking about freedom.

"What did it sound like?" her mother asked the next morning.

"It sounded like he was talking about saving the country," Anita replied.

"Well, that was the first step," her mother said.

She wanted to ask her teacher what it all meant, but he would probably laugh at her because dreams were just part of the imagination. As Anita got older she started to wonder if she was even dreaming at all. Maybe she was traveling through space and time and seeing things as they really were.

One night, Anita dreamed of herself. She was sitting in a room, ready to give a speech. She was surrounded by people who were keeping their distance and letting her collect her thoughts. She had her mom's old record player in the room with her. Sam Cooke was playing. She was thinking about her mother and about a T-Rex. About how everyone was just trying to survive and be happy despite a world that was working against them. When the song was over, she turned off the record player, picked up her speech, and walked onto a balcony. Outside there were reporters and cameras and millions of people cheering. She put her hand on a Bible and repeated the words that were said to her. She turned and looked out across the lawn, across the crowd that stretched from the White House to the Lincoln Memorial. She then gave her speech, which was about freedom, and it sounded like it was about freedom.

When she woke up, she told her mother about the dream she had. Her mother liked this dream very much.

Outroductions

I was sitting on a park bench, re-reading my stories, when the man from my future came to me a third time.

"How is it?" he asked me.

I told him I didn't know.

He read it, and told me, "It's not finished yet."

I didn't know what other stories to include, and I told him that. I told him it feels finished.

"It needs a litmus test," he said.

I just looked at him, puzzled.

"It needs a litmus test to see if the world is changing in the right direction. A story that is ahead of its time but, when read fifty years from now, is so out of place and time that no one understands what it's about."

I still didn't get it.

"Do you know who Bill Gaines is?" he asked.

My silence told him that I didn't.

"Back in my days, Bill Gaines was a man who made comic books. Not the superhero books you think of when you think of comic books. He made comic books about crime, horror, war, and romance. He made comic books about humans, sometimes bad humans, but humans nonetheless.

"Back in my days there was also this man named Fredric Wertham. Fredric Wertham was a psychologist who believed comics like the one Bill Gaines made were poisoning kids' minds. Making them violent. Making them criminals. Even making them fall in love with people that Fredric Wertham felt they shouldn't be falling in love with.

"All Bill Gaines had on his side was stories, artists, and kids. Fredric Wertham, however, had everyone else.

"Fredric Wertham screamed his beliefs to everyone else. He wrote magazine articles and even a book called *The Seduction of the Innocent*. He made people afraid, and, if you make people afraid, you can change things in terrible ways before they realize how terrible the changes are.

"A code was established in 1954. It was called the Comics Code. All comic books had to adhere to the code or else comic book distributors would not sell them. Under the Code, all comic books had to have good triumphing over evil, no excessive violence, no werewolves or vampires, no seduction, and many other 'no's, not leaving a lot of room for much of anything else.

"The Code targeted every book Bill Gaines put out, and Bill Gaines tried to fight back against the code. It didn't take long for Bill Gaines to stop publishing comic books altogether. However, he decided to focus instead on a book called *Mad Magazine*.

"The last comic Bill Gaines published was released in 1956, two years after the Comics Code was established. The comic was called *Incredible Science Fiction* #33. The last story in that last comic was a piece called 'Judgement Day.' It was about an astronaut from Earth who was sent to the planet of Cybrinia, a planet populated by robots, to see if they were worthy of joining Earth's great Galactic Republic. When he toured Cybernia, he saw that it was a segregated society, where orange robots and blue robots lived in different parts of town, worked different jobs, and went to different schools.

"Since Cybernia had a segregated society, the astronaut was not able to allow them into Earth's great Galactic Republic. In the final panel the astronaut removed his helmet, and the reader saw that he was a black man."

The man from my future paused and waited for my reaction. I didn't have one.

"And that's the litmus test. Back in 1956, the Comics Code rejected that story unless the astronaut was changed to a white man."

I asked the man from my future why that change needed to be made.

"The Comics Code authorities had various reasons. The most ridiculous one was because the astronaut was sweating in the panel. But the reality was, back in 1956, back in a time when black men and women lived in separate parts of town and worked at separate jobs and attended separate schools, people simply weren't OK with the very idea of a black man being an astronaut.

"Gaines fought back and eventually won. The comic was printed as originally intended. And now, when most people who didn't grow up back then read the story, they simply don't get it. The story is so out of place and time that they simply don't understand what it's about."

I nodded my head and understood what the man from my

future wanted. I set about creating a litmus test.

Try Looking Ahead

When Charles was five, his father got him a bicycle, a real bicycle with two wheels, an upgrade from his current tricycle. His father put a helmet on his head and patted him on the back, and said, "You just pedal, and I'll hold the seat to keep you steady. Just try looking ahead and you'll be fine."

Charles put his feet on the pedals and started moving his legs and the real bicycle with two wheels started moving and his father was holding onto the seat, keeping Charles steady. Charles tried looking ahead, but after some time he looked back and saw his father waving in the distance. Charles got scared and swerved and his bike slid out from under him and he hit the ground, hard.

"That's OK," his father told him. "Just try again. Look ahead. Always look ahead."

Before getting on his bike, Charles closed his eyes and tried to look ahead. He tried to see what would come next.

―――――――――

When Charles was eight, his father signed him up for baseball. All of his friends were playing, and he wanted to play with them, even though he never cared much for baseball. Charles's father took him to the batting cage to teach him how to hit, even though Charles's father never really knew how to play baseball either. But his father tried to teach him anyway, handing him a helmet and a bat and giving him the only advice he could think of, "When you're waiting for the ball to come, just try looking ahead. The moment that ball comes out, swing as hard as you can."

Charles gripped the bat and stared ahead at the pitcher, and, as soon as a ball popped out, he swung his bat as hard as he could. He probably could have swung his bat three more times before the ball actually reached him. Charles stood there and watched the ball pass him by. He looked back at his dad, who shrugged, and suggested, "Try swinging later, I guess."

Charles looked ahead and swung later, but he still missed. He eventually hit a ball, and he also eventually realized that he didn't care much for baseball.

––––––––––

When Charles was 13, his father bought him a telescope. None of his friends had telescopes so it took Charles some time to warm up to the idea that he had one. Eventually, he took his telescope out back and pointed it up to the sky and tried to find something, anything, worth looking at up close. He couldn't find a thing.

Charles told his father that space was boring. His father told him that he'd love him no matter what, unconditionally, through thick and thin...but if Charles ever said that space was boring again, he'd have to move out.

Charles laughed because he knew his father was joking, but then his father put down his book, and said, "Seriously, though, space isn't boring. Space is amazing. Did you ever wonder why the moon rises every night and sets every morning?"

"Because it's revolving around the earth," Charles replied. Everyone knew that.

"But do you know what that means?"

Charles started to open his mouth but then realized that he didn't know what that meant.

"The moon is revolving around the earth because it's falling into the earth."

Charles thought about that for a second, and then asked, "But why doesn't it hit us?"

"Because the earth's falling into the sun, causing the moon to always miss the earth. All of the planets in our solar system are falling into the sun, but they're always missing because the sun is falling into the center of our galaxy. The sun never gets there, however, because the center of our galaxy is always falling into the center of our local group of galaxies, which, in turn, is always falling toward our local supercluster of groups, which, in turn, is always falling into the center of the universe.

"Everything you can see is always falling toward something. And the fact that most things aren't hitting anything is one of the most amazing, non-boring things you will ever witness."

Charles imagined his own feet, pressed against the floor of his house. He realized that if the floor were to disappear, he'd fall until he hit another floor. He never realized that he was always falling into the earth and that the only thing stopping him from getting hurt was the ground that was constantly stopping his fall.

Charles's father saw the confusion on his son's face. "Don't think about falling," he said. "Just try looking ahead."

Charles went back outside and peered into his telescope. He spent an hour staring at a giant rock that was falling toward him, always missing.

When Charles was 16, he told his father a secret. His father made a joke at first but then hugged him and told him that no matter what happens next, always try looking ahead.

———————

When Charlie was 18, her father bought her a car. It wasn't a great car. It was actually in terrible shape. It was ten years old and had a rearview mirror that fell off and a door that rattled and a radio that couldn't play MP3s and a rear defrost that wouldn't defrost. But it was all Charlie's dad could afford, and he knew that she would need a car in college.

"Sometimes you'll feel the need to get away, I'm sure," he told her. "And when you do, just get in this car and try looking ahead. Drive all the way home if you want and never look back. I'll be here with the light on."

Charlie drove all the way home only once, during her first year of school, when she was feeling incredibly homesick and alone. She spent the whole night talking to her father outside the house, with her old telescope pointed up to a giant rock that was falling toward her but always missing her.

She remembered why she went to college and drove back the next morning.

She looked ahead for the next eight years.

———————

When Charlie was 30, her girlfriend came to visit her lab. Charlie showed her the most recent pictures of bright and beautiful objects trillions of miles away that were falling into other bright and beautiful objects but always missing because everything was always falling into something else. Charlie told her girlfriend that even right now they're falling into each other but that, since they both weigh about the same, their falling sort of cancels out.

"What if I were heavier?" Charlie's girlfriend asked.

Charlie thought about that for a second, laughed, and said, "You'd have to meet my dad first."

"I'm just trying to look ahead," Charlie's girlfriend replied. "Just like you always told me to do."

_____

When Charlie was 40, she took her wife and daughter to her father's sixtieth birthday party. It was at the old house, which hadn't changed much over the years. At some point that night, she looked outside the window to see her daughter standing on her toes, trying to look into her old telescope. Charlie was about to go outside with her daughter but saw that her dad was already out there, undoubtedly telling her daughter about large objects falling into them but always missing.

Undoubtedly telling her to always try looking ahead.

_____

When Charlie was 55, she sat down next to her father, who was lying in bed, eyes closed and breathing steady.

She kissed his forehead, thanked him for everything, and told him that no matter what happens next, to try looking ahead.

_____

When Charles was five he opened his eyes.

"What did you see?" his father asked.

"I saw me riding this bike," Charles answered.

About the Author

Jason Rodriguez is a comic book writer and editor. The books he has edited or contributed to have been nominated for an Eisner Award and 10 Harvey Awards. Jason is currently editing a three-book series of anthologies about colonial New England and the Mid-Atlantic region for Fulcrum Publishing. His first sci-fi book, *Try Looking Ahead*, was released in June 2015 from Rosarium Publishing. November 2015 will see the release of his anthology, *APB: Artists Against Police Brutality*, co-edited with Bill Campbell and John Jennings, from Rosarium Publishing as well as the 10th anniversary hardcover edition of *Elk's Run*. Jason lives in Arlington, VA with his wife and a rotating collection of pets. You can usually find him on a street corner, staring out into the future.

Other Books by Jason Rodriguez

Available:

Postcards: Trust Stories That Never Happened (Editor)

Elk's Run (Editor)

Colonial Comics: New England, 1620-1750 (Editor)

District Comics: An Unconventional History of Washington DC (Contributing Writer)

Once Upon a Time Machine (Contributing Writer)

Upcoming:

Elk's Run: 10th Anniversary Hardcover (Editor, November, 2015)

APB: Artists Against Police Brutality (Editor, November, 2015)

Colonial Comics: New England, 1750-1775 (Editor, April 2016)

Colonial Comics: Mid-Atlantic, 1607-1775 (Editor, April 2017)

C:\> ENDTRANSMISSION 010011000110111101101
1110110101100100000001000001011010000110010
10110000101100100